CHRIS WADE

GHOSTLY TALES

Ghostly Tales
by Chris Wade

Text Copyright of Chris Wade, 2025

ISBN: 978-1-326-76707-5

All rights reserved. No part of this publication may be reproduced, stored in a retrieval system, or transmitted in any form or by any means, electronic, mechanical, photocopy, recording or otherwise, without prior written permission of the copyright owner. Nor can it be circulated in any form of binding or cover other than that in which it is published and without similar condition including this condition being imposed on a subsequent purchaser.

Ghostly Tales

by Chris Wade

CONTENTS

The Old Man

The Abandoned Asylum

The Lady in the Field

The Singing Spirit

About Chris Wade

THE OLD MAN

It was the summer of 1997 and I was 12 years old. Days were long as the cliché goes, and the sun seemed ever present, which to me it was. I would wake up completely refreshed at 8 in the morning every single day during those school holidays, and the sun would already be burning in the sky, blazing in through my bedroom window, scorchingly hot through the glass, and through the curtains which could not hope to block out its immovable glow. When the day was through, and I'd exhausted myself completely, I would call it a day and head to my bedroom, usually around 9:30. The sun, even then, would still be sitting in the sky; admittedly dimmer but still present, still painting its vibrant colours. So quite literally my summer was eternally light, eternally sunny, an endless and glorious summer. Well, it was glorious for a little while. Then there was a shift, literally overnight, when I came across the old man's house. Nothing was ever the same after that. Not really…

But let me go back first. I was in the first year of high school and while I can't say I hated my time there, I was hardly in love with it either. I wasn't bullied thank god, but then again I didn't have that many friends either, though that was more out of choice to be honest. I never felt the need to mix with and be around a lot of people, and my happiness has never really relied on anyone else being there. OK, I could enjoy playing with others at break time, and after school I did like to go to the park and climb up trees and hide in the woods with the local kids, but for the most part I was an introverted child who liked his own company, who loved nothing more than sitting under a tree in the park and writing stories or drawing weird pictures. My friends would find me there and look at my pictures with amusement, but they never wanted to sit down and join in. No, they'd go off and play football. It's not that they found me odd or weird, just different. "Oh, that's Tony, he sits alone a lot." That kind of thing. They accepted me for who I was, which was a good thing for a 12 year old kid.

It was around four weeks into the six week holidays that I found myself getting even less interested in playing with the other kids, and I was roaming around town more and more, always alone, always exploring odd little corners I had never found before. On the outskirts of the town, past the housing estates, I found an old factory. I had fun one day investigating it all. Earlier in the month I had found my dad's old Polaroid camera, so I took it along with me and captured some creepy pictures of abandoned corridors and rusty old machines. I'm not sure what the factory had actually made all those years ago, before it was an empty cavernous place, but there was enough machinery to suggest it was something pretty heavy duty. I went back a second day, when I found a homeless guy drunk in one of the old staff rooms. When he saw me in the doorway he threw an empty bottle in a rage, and it smashed hard against the wall beside me. He was about to get up, scrambling clumsily to his unsteady feet, so I ran away as fast as I could. In retrospect I realise that the old drunk probably didn't even get up off the floor. That would have required too much energy and effort. He more than likely just wanted to scare me away, not hurt me. Anyway, his aggression and foul mouthed ranting was enough to put me off ever going back to the old factory.

One day, I was sat at the dining table having a late breakfast my mum. Thick, crispy toast, with plenty of thick jam. My dad was in the kitchen too, eating a speedy bowl of cornflakes before heading off to work. After all, even though I was off for six weeks, he still had to go to work. He didn't mind though. He was a good man and he knew he had to work to provide for me, my mum and my sister Claire. Speaking of Claire, she was 17 at this point in time and I barely saw her all summer. She was staying with her boyfriend Luke and his parents. Me and my sister didn't get along too well, so let's just say that I didn't mind her not being around.

It's funny, but I have a very specific memory of me sitting there with the jam on toast, with my mum reading a magazine opposite me at the table.

"So what are you getting up to today, Tony?" she asked. I recall her eyes didn't shift from the magazine, which must have been terribly riveting I am sure.

"I don't know actually," I said with a hint of vagueness.

"Why don't you play with your friends? Are they up at the park today, do you know?"

"They will be," I said, nibbling my toast. "But I don't feel like playing with them today. I fancy a day to myself."

"Not the computer games again I hope," she said, peering up for a second before going back to her reading.

"No, I'm bored of them to be honest. I'm going for a wander."

"Where to?"

"Oh I don't know," I said. "There's only a couple of weeks left of the holidays, so I'm going to go exploring. Pack some sandwiches, have a picnic somewhere." I gazed out of the window. The sun shone in my eyes. "The weather's perfect for it."

Mum nodded, and after sighing, either out of boredom or contentment (it was hard to tell), she looked up at me.

"Well, just stay safe OK?"

I nodded.

"Promise?" she said firmly.

"Promise," I said.

She smiled warmly at me. I still remember that smile very clearly. It was one of genuine love. At that moment my dad left the kitchen and said ta-ta before heading off out of the front door, seen but not heard as he closed it behind him. As I finished my toast, I caught sight of him getting into his car and heading off for work.

About 15 minutes later I was out of the door too. It was around 10:30 and I had a little back pack over my shoulder containing a couple of sandwiches, a drink and some crisps. What did I do first? Well, I started walking, heading out of my neighbourhood and round the corner. Looking around me at the various houses and listening to the bird song, I lost track of where I was heading and in no time I found myself on a street I wasn't familiar with. It seemed impossible that there was a road so close to my house I had never set foot on, but I swear that I had never been there before.

It was so different to the other places in town that it immediately struck me as very odd. The houses seemed older than the ones only around the corner, and there was no one around on the street, no one crossing the road, no one walking the path. Not even anyone pottering around in their gardens. Literally, there was no one around.

There was something else strange, too. Though it was a sunny day, it seemed to me that this street wasn't getting as much sun as the others. That seems silly I know, but to my eyes it was much greyer, much dimmer than everywhere else. It was as if the place was shrouded somehow, like giant unseen curtains were blocking out the sun rays. Still, it was pleasant in its own way, just a little off centre if you know what I mean.

I walked on for a while and found myself coming towards a house which intrigued me. It was bigger than the others and seemed a little more run down. There were trees in the garden but for some reason they were bare. Perhaps they were dead, because given this was the middle of the summer they should have been full of green leaves. But no, they were skeletal, which was immediately strange to me. There were bushes in the garden too, and some ivy over the front wall. Still, none of it seemed in bloom. It was all just there, existing, growing against all odds. The gate was rusty too, and there were even some cob webs over it, as if no one had been in or out in years. Did anyone even live there, I wondered.

Gazing up at the house itself, I saw it had four windows on the front, two upstairs, two down. The curtains in each were pulled shut, blocking out the day, and the front door was green with a foggy window pane on it. I stood still and looked at the place carefully. Something about it stuck out other than its creepiness. As I looked closely, it was then I saw the curtain on the right window start to part ever so slightly. I saw a hand, an old and frail looking hand, pulling it to one side. Then I saw a man's face, but the room behind him was so dark I couldn't make him out clearly.

Feeling uneasy, I began to back away as the old man in the window looked my way. I then looked around the street. Still, there was not a soul around. I was the only living person there. The street was deserted. Looking back at the old house, I saw the old man's face was gone and the curtain was once again closed. Hurriedly, feeling a little panicky inside, I began to walk away. I peered back over my shoulder at the house and felt a shiver up my spine. Quickening my pace, I found myself off the street in no time at all, returning back to the ones I knew well and was more comfortable with.

I spent the rest of the day in the woods, climbing trees, going over little bridges and sitting down to eat my snacks and write my thoughts in my journal. Still, I thought back to the old man, the sight of his bony hand pulling the curtain, his featureless face in the window, eyes that I could not see but could feel upon me. Weird.

The next day I headed out early again. I had my toast at the table and watched as my mother read over a magazine, a different one. This time I took my tape walkman and listened to music as I headed down the road. The first tape was the Sabotage album by Black Sabbath. I distinctly remember turning the corner off my street as Am I Going Insane? played in my ears on the head phones, which were too big for my head and looked rather ridiculous. Still, I didn't care. The weather was good and so was the music.

As the song faded out (and I know the timing perfectly, as I later wrote it all down in my journal), I found that I had turned on to the street I had stumbled upon the day before. Eerily, the song in question ends with maniacal sped up laughter, and it seemed fitting somehow that I found myself on the eerily quiet street with the mad guffawing playing in my ears.

Turning off the tape player, I put it in my back pack and settled the ear phones around my neck.

I was wearing a red cap on that day to keep the blazing sun out of my face. Not that I needed it on that fusty street of course, because as on the day before, I found it much dimmer than the rest of town.

I walked on, slowly and carefully, listening to the silence on the street. That was another thing, even the birds were quiet around that part of town, so much so that I could barely hear any. It was as if the whole place was on mute. Still, it was oddly comforting to find a road where no else seemed to go and which was as quiet as this one.

It was then I found myself once more in front of the weird house. This time, though, I noticed that the front door was slightly open ajar. Intrigued, I stepped slowly to the gate, which was also open a tiny bit. It was as if I was being invited inside.

Pushing it aside, the gate creaked loudly as I made my way through. Going up the path very slowly, my shoes squeaking with each step, I got closer to the front door. It was dark green, and had clearly been painted so many years ago, judging by the flakiness peeling off and revealing the brown wood beneath. Though I was nervous, something drew me further in. What it was exactly I could not decide. More than a curiosity, I was pulled in for another reason which eluded me completely.

Getting to the door, I raised my hand automatically and without any thought. About to knock, I found that the door opened itself, very slowly, and eerily so with a loud creaking sound. As it swung open, revealed to me was a long dark corridor. There was no light in there, but I could see a dim glow coming from the room to the right, so I figured there must have been a lamp on. Still unsure why I was doing this, I stepped into the house and began to walk down the dark corridor. The further in I got, the more curious I began to feel. I heard music playing from the room to the right, music which to my young ears sounded like Noel Coward - and in fact probably was.

I got nearer to the unseen room and the music - tinny as it was, and clearly playing from an old record player - grew louder. Entering the room, I saw there was a dim lamp on in one corner by an old TV which was switched off. On its blank, black screen I could see the room reflected; the record player on the small table, the lamp shade, and most importantly of all, an old man sitting in a corner arm chair. He was very clear to me, even in a reflection as frosty as this one; his face smiling, his clothes dull but well fitting, his thin hair combed to one side. Turning from the television screen, I looked towards the chair. To my surprise and disbelief, I saw it was empty. The record continued to slowly spin on the table beside it, but there was quite clearly no one sitting in that chair. And yet I had seen an old man in the reflection, snugly sitting there, his hands on the chair arms, his small body comfortable against the high back.

Looking back to the TV screen, once again I could see him there, planted in the chair like a permanent fixture, like a wax work of a smiling old man who had been moulded into it. I looked closer at his reflection and saw that his foot was tapping to the jaunty music, his head bobbing too, ever so slightly.

Turning my face away quickly, I looked back to the chair in the corner. Once again, it was revealed to me that there was no one there. I listened carefully. Beneath the music, only just audible, was the sound of a foot tapping on a carpeted floor. The old man was enjoying the music, still. Glaring at the chair, I could almost see him there in the flesh before me, feel his presence, smell his old man scents, the soap he might have scrubbed himself with. Still, physically at least he wasn't there.

Then the song ended and the record crackled on, the needle reaching the end of the vinyl. It stuck there for a few seconds and made a popping sound, before eventually going silent and stopping all together. The room fell into a terrible silence. I stood in disbelief for a few moments and wasn't sure what to do next.

Then my mind was made up for me. Behind me in the doorway a woman entered the room all of a sudden. She was an attractive woman with blonde hair, aged around 40 to 45, maybe older, I wasn't sure. She stood there by the open door, a hint of light in a dark, dingy room, her red lip stick glowing from her full mouth. She was both mumsy to me but also terribly attractive.

"Who are you?" she said, her tone harsh and angry. The moment was spoilt. The beautiful woman had turned on me. "What are you doing here?"

"I'm sorry. I just came in. The door was open. I'll leave now." Feeling like I was about to cry, I went to leave the room. But as I moved across to the doorway, the woman held up her hand and stopped me dead in my tracks.

"No, wait!" she said suddenly. Her hand touched my chest. I was as still as a statue. Going down to her knees slowly, and with an expression that was unsettling, she gazed right into my face. She was so close I could smell her minty breath and her sweet perfume. I could even feel her breath on my face as she inspected me closely.

"What's wrong?" I said, feeling genuinely scared.

"Well," she said, her eyes drifting off slightly, and then all together. After a few seconds, she came back to her senses and looked at me with clarity, as if she had just been freed from a hypnotic spell. "I'm sorry young man, it's just that... well... you look like somebody. You look like them a lot actually. It's... it's quite remarkable."

She stood up straight and leaned back on the wall behind her. Still, the woman looked down at me with startled eyes, though admittedly her mood was much calmer now. Gazing back at her, I found my eyes drifting to the right of the woman's body. My attention was taken by a framed picture, an old fading image of a young boy standing in front of the very house I was in at that moment. I looked closer at the face of the boy and realised that he not only looked like me, but that he could have been my twin. It was remarkable, the resemblance was disturbing, and I found myself unable to move or speak.

Seeing my haunted expression, the woman followed my gaze and turned her eyes to the picture. She looked at it for a few seconds, and then her gaze went to the ground, the brown carpet beneath our feet.

"He was my brother," she said, her voice filling the muffled silence, the suffocating atmosphere. "He died a long time ago. He was five years older than me. I barely remember him now. All I have is this picture."

She looked back at the picture, her eyes tearing up, and then she glanced at me.

"What happened to him?" I dared to ask. It was almost a desperate attempt to break the silence, to move things along so I could leave.

"Oh, he died," she said with a bluntness. "My dad took that picture. He loved my brother. He really did. That's why he never moved from this house. My mother left soon after my brother's death and we never saw her much after that. She's dead now, but she was dead to us years ago, decades ago in fact. I don't think she got over my brother's death. Neither did my dad. That's why he clung to this place. He took that picture in front of this house… all those years ago."

There was a silence while she looked at the picture. I nervously played with my hands and suddenly felt a cold chill up my back.

"Does your father still live here?" I asked.

"Well he did up until last week," she replied. "Until he passed away. I'm here to clear things up, get things in order."

The woman looked at me, and I saw worry come upon her face, alarmingly so in fact. She was looking at me with concern.

"Are you OK, young man?" she asked, moving closer to me. "You've gone all pale. Are you feeling all right?"

"Yes," I said, "I got to go. My mother will be wondering where I am."

I moved quickly and ran past the lady in the doorway. Dashing down the corridor, I felt her come out to watch me as I left the house.

"Take care!" she said from behind me as I entered the warm air. I sprinted down the front path and exited the garden through the still open gate, its rusty hinges creaking as I passed through and entered the street.

As I ran on, I tried to resist the temptation to look back at the house, but I found it too hard. Peering over my shoulder, running still, I saw the woman. She was standing in the doorway, her face wistful, her eyes distant. But then I looked at the window, the curtains parted, and I found my eyes directly upon the face of the old man. He was looking out at me, his features not clear to me, his eyes impossible to see, but his longing for his long dead son almost too much to bear. My heart was pounding and I had a suffocating desire to leave that street and never come back. My mood didn't even begin to calm until I was back in my neighbourhood.

For the rest of the holidays I stayed away from the old house. I spent the rest of the couple of weeks I had left at home, drawing, writing, watching TV, and playing my computer games. Though I couldn't bring myself to go back to that weird place, it never left my mind. Nor did the old man, who was clearly heartbroken still all those years on, even after he had departed the earth as a living being. That's why he was drawn to me, why he was trying to lure me into his house. Is it possible he actually thought I was his boy, or was he merely comforted by my resemblance to him? I never found out, but I was sure it was the former. There was such desperation in his aura.

All these years on, I still think of the woman and the way she stared at me in the living room, and the faceless old man, so sad, and yet so sure that I was the son he had lost all those years ago. I'm a man now, and I live very far away from the town I grew up in. My parents still have their house there of course, and every time I go to visit them I consider heading across town to that dim, dull street. But I never do. I can never bring myself to go in that direction for fear of what I might see. How old will the woman be now? Will she too be dead? I'd rather not know. I'd rather keep the image of them both in the distant past, she in the doorway, he in the window parting the curtain. It's a past so distant and an image so unreal to me that it feels like some strange dream. And that's how I'd rather think of it, like some strange dream.

THE ABANDONED ASYLUM

It was a chilly Saturday in early March, perhaps very late February. It was a Saturday, and like on most Saturdays my wife, my daughter and I decided to go out for a family trip somewhere. Nowhere in particular in mind, we got in the car, my wife driving, me in the back seat and my ten year old daughter in the front passenger. Don't ask me why we sit that way, and why I end up in the back like a toddler, but that's the way it is and I don't really mind. In fact, I rather like it.

Seating arrangements aside, we set off out on to the road and chatted as my wife made her way round various streets and neighbourhoods. In the end, after a half hour or so, we wound up near a woodland we'd frequented in the past. It's a fairly thick woodland in the summer, though given this was very late winter the trees were bare. About 100 metres in there's a small playground for kids, gated and fenced off from the trees. We locked the car and headed slowly and calmly towards the path leading into the wood, aiming for the playground, our coats fastened up, me with my flat cap on and hands in pockets.

My daughter, as children often do, ran ahead of us to get to the park, pushing open the gate excitedly and getting straight on to a swing. Me and my wife joined her in the park, sitting on a bench and watching our little girl swing away. She asked her mother to push her, so my wife got up and did as she was told, pushing her lightly on her back. I watched her soar higher, her little feet in trainers against the cloudy white sky.

It was then my gaze drifted to the left of the park, and I could see something through the bare branches of the trees there. I sat forward on the bench and focused on what I was looking at. I saw it was a house. Well, not quite a house, but a mansion, a huge, expansive place. I stood up and moved closer, very slowly, cautiously in fact even from such a distance, and the further I went the more clearly the mansion became to me. It appeared to be abandoned. Most of the windows were broken, some not there at all, others covered by wooden boards.

"Come and look at this!" I said over my shoulder, still looking at the mansion, captivated by it somehow. My wife joined me slowly, and I felt her behind me looking at the house. I could still hear the squeaking chains on the swing on which my daughter sat and went back and forth.

We both gazed at the house, its Victorian structure, its hugeness, but also its unsettling nature. Indeed, there was something off about it, something creepy. There was no life within it, at least not of the human kind.

Retrieving my daughter, the three of us left the wood and approached the house. Still, the closer we got, the more weird the place felt. It had an aura, an undefinable aura which left me speechless and uncomfortable. I made a couple of jokes about it to lighten the mood, but still I felt unnerved, unsettled.

Standing right before it, it was clear that the council had erected some feeble metal fencing around the mansion, but there were huge gaps, which meant that anyone could easily cut through and go inside on to the grounds. Feeling brave, I decided to slip through the fence and approach it. My wife told me not to, but I ignored her. My daughter followed me too, and we made our way across the grass leading to the entrance of the mansion.

"It's spooky here," my daughter said quietly. I agreed with a firm nod, my eyes on the house which was now closer to me than I felt comfortable with, its huge, imposing structure towering over me. It was as if it was looking at me, looming over me as it was, considering me, regarding me with amusement.

I stood at the front door which was all boarded up. There was no way inside, not on the ground level anyway, and if a squatter or homeless person did want to go in they'd have had to climb to the first or second floor and get in through a window. That said, the place gave off an atmosphere of being completely devoid of human life. There might have been pigeons nesting in the old roof, or rats scurrying in the floorboards, possibly other wildlife dwelling silently within, but there was certainly no living person in there.

It was then I got the oddest feeling, as if I could hear the chattering of people, dozens of them, without actually hearing them for real... if that makes sense. I heard the voices, through it was as if they were not audible to ordinary ears. It was like they had been presented to me from somewhere else, an echo of laughter from years ago perhaps, the voices of people long gone. Gone where, however, I did not know.

I suddenly felt cold, colder than I had through the rest of our time in the wood and the park, and I had a sudden urge to leave. Grabbing my daughter's hand, I backed away from the old house.

"Come on," I said. She wanted to stay longer and investigate more, but I was having none of it. The place felt dark and alive with something I didn't understand.

Moving away, and heading back to the other side of the fence, I saw my wife standing on the path beside the old mansion. It was then that I saw over her shoulder a figure. At first it was so small and far in the distance that I couldn't make much out. My wife saw me looking past her, so she turned too and caught sight of the mysterious person. When they got closer, I saw they were walking very slowly with their hands in their pockets. Their head was covered by a hood and they were moving so subtly it didn't seem possible that any living human being could do so with such little purpose. It wasn't a relaxed stroll, it was more like a floating movement, but depressed and lifeless, a walk without any feeling or real direction. When the person got nearer to us, its silhouette much clearer, we began to feel, admittedly, a little scared, and terribly nervous. Though having no real aim, it seemed to be heading towards us regardless, whether we were there or not.

"Come on, let's get back to the car," my wife said, and we did so. Moving speedily than before, every few seconds as we made our way back to the park and the woodland I found myself looking over my shoulder. And there it was, the figure, still walking ever so slowly, now right beside the old abandoned mansion. When we got to the entry way to the playground I turned once more and saw the figure had vanished. All I could see now was the old house, that Victorian abode I knew so little of and was now curious to investigate.

Later that evening when we were all safely at home, the fire on and the TV quietly flickering away in the corner, I went on my computer to research abandoned houses in the area we had visited. The search results sent a shiver down my spine. It turned out that the building was an old abandoned mental asylum. It first opened in the Victorian era, at the back end of it in fact, after a millionaire sold it to the council. It functioned as a bedlam for over seventy five years, and at one point was notorious for its ill treatment of, if not downright cruelty towards, its patients. It had closed in the 1970s and had drifted into obscurity. The council had no plans to do anything with it, neither demolish nor sell it to developers. So there it stood, a reminder of another era, a house of bad memories.

Leaning back in my chair, reading this information, I then thought of the hooded figure. Who was that person? Were they alive, a real living person, or an apparition, a vision of someone who had once been an inmate at the asylum and now spent his eternity roaming the path around it, aimlessly repeating the same movement, day in day out, forever. At first I thought such a theory utterly mad, but then I realised it wasn't so crazy after all. Maybe he had been released from the asylum and never quite moved on, and longed for his former home for the rest of his days, a longing that continued into the after life.

Chilled, I turned off the PC and headed over to my corner arm chair. I leant back and closed my eyes, the sound of the TV strangely soothing, and the lamp beside me glowing comfortingly. It was then with eyes closed and listening to the sound of my own gentle breathing, feeling my ribs go in and out with each deep, slow breath, that I swore I heard those voices from the old mansion, or should I say the abandoned asylum, those chattering voices, echoing on through the decades, people now long gone from the physical world, but existing on some other plane. I didn't share my thoughts with my wife or anyone else for that matter, but after that night I often thought about them, the patients of the old abandoned asylum, whispering to each other in the dark.

THE LADY IN THE FIELD

I was excited about my new job, the possibilities that awaited me in the establishment that was - for whatever reasons they had - about to take me on, and all the new people I was going to meet, work with, and hopefully make friends of. What I wasn't so excited about, however, was the long drive I would have to take every day of my working week. As I realised, to my rather hysterical sense of neurotic horror, much of the journey would have to be undertaken on main roads - and very busy main roads at that; main roads notorious for their ever-flowing sea of traffic. I had been on those roads before in the past, when I was in my early twenties, often with an ex-girlfriend or casual partner, on our way to some place for some unknown reason, a place now forgotten to me. It had been years since I had been on those roads, and as far as I knew, and had indeed heard, they were worse than ever before.

I tried to put all these fears aside, because I was genuinely enthused about the new job. In truth, the change in my employment status had come at the perfect time. I had been jobless for six months, and given I had some savings in my account - left to me by my late auntie, no word of a lie - I could not claim anything on the unemployment. Six months doesn't seem like a very long time, but in terms of money and an ever depleting bank balance, it can feel like an eternity. Adding to that of course was the loss of my personal confidence. Quite naturally, I began fearing that I would begin to rot in my feckless life style, a listless ghost of a man, little more than a sunken-cheeked, hollow-eyed lost soul queueing up for my fortnightly pay-out at the dole office until old age wore me down to mere bones and flaps of skin. Getting the job and "aceing" the interview, as some people would say, gave me a much needed boost.

The day before I was going to start my new job, I bumped into my neighbour, John, just as I was pushing the recycle bin to the front of the garden.

"Jack, how are you?" he said, friendly as ever, and only half drunk this time, which was unusual for a Sunday night. For some reason, he was always more inebriated on Sundays than any other day. That said, old John was retired and it was up to him what he did with his weekends - and his weekdays, too, for that matter.

I told him about my new job, and informed him that I wasn't exactly looking forward to the long drive on all those busy main roads. It was then, in an oddly alarming moment, that his eyes lit up, and a grin appeared on his face. It was a smile intending to be friendly, but it seemed somehow sinister to me on that warm evening.

"Wait there!" he said, before dashing inside as quickly as he could. I have to say that for a fellow so advanced in years he was surprisingly quick and light-footed. For a few moments I stood with my hands in the pockets of my loose jogging bottoms, the Sunday relaxing wear which had seen better days, and whistled as I waited. Around a minute or so later John returned, and over the fence that separated our gardens, he handed me a piece of paper. On it he had drawn a map, rather simply so upon first glance, offering me an alternative route to my new job. It was ten miles away, and the only way I knew how to get there was by the afore-mentioned main roads. But old John - good old John I should say - clearly knew of an alternative route.

"This will cut an hour off your journey," he said, winking, "maybe even more."

I thanked him and shook his hand, before returning indoors to unwind for the evening. He went indoors too, audibly opening another can of beer before closing the door. I couldn't help but smile to myself.

Surprisingly so given my mounting nerves, I slept well that night. Before going to bed I had hung my work clothes over the bedside table. Thinking ahead, I had bought a couple of new suits so I would look my best for my new colleagues; not that I was obsessed with pleasing people you understand, but I didn't want to show up on my first day looking like a derelict in an unmade bed.

I awoke nice and early, feeling optimistic and only a little bit nervous about meeting an office full of new people. After my shower I went downstairs and had some toast with the radio on, though I didn't listen to a word of what was said. Instead, I found myself looking over the map old John had drawn for me, and I saw that most of the route was through country back roads.

"I hope you're right, John," I said, biting my toast before heading for the front door, leaving the radio on to play to an empty dining room.

I laid the map down on the seat beside me and set off down the road. Following his directions to the tiniest detail - not that there were that many details mind you - before I knew it I was heading down obscure back streets and weird little country roads. I had lived in that house for two years and had no idea I was so close to so much greenery. Such is the sad truth of working in the city. Being preoccupied by the grey metropolis and those imposing skyscrapers, you miss out on all of

God's green and pleasant land, all of which is there around the corner to discover and explore.

A little way into the trip, I found myself going down what I felt to be a particularly obscure part of the country. Sticking to the road, there were two huge, seemingly endless fields at either side of me. They went on for some time before coming to a turn off, leading on to a straight road lined with thick and luscious trees. It was early September, the air was still warm, and though Autumn was starting to rear her head, the weather was still pleasant. The green had not yet even begun turning to brown.

When the trees cleared, I found the car turning a corner, a sharpish corner in fact, which opened up a large field to my right which immediately felt different to the others. Quite how, I did not know, but there was an eeriness to it that was not apparent in the previous greenery. Though not covered by any trees or growth, it somehow seemed darker here, the grass more dull, and the one tree which I spotted standing up on the hill in the distance, alone and lonesome, already losing its leaves. There was something unusual about this place, but how unusual I wouldn't find out until later.

And then I saw it. I use the word "it" because no other word will suffice, nor more correctly summarise my emotions upon first viewing. What was it? Well, when I focused my eyes as best as I could, I saw it was a scarecrow, propped up wonkily at the far end of the field beside a fence which led to a dark patch of forest. It was very far away, but even from that distance I could see it was a scarecrow. Well, that's what it first appeared to be. For some reason, even though it was little more than a dot to me from the road, I found myself drawn to it; eerily magnetic it was, even though there was nothing even remotely interesting or intriguing about it in any way. But still, I could not keep my gaze off it. I could see that the actual figure of the scarecrow was black, but its head a sharply contrasting white. Apart from that there was nothing else to make it stick out to me. And yet…

Finally, after what felt like an age, I found the car drifting round the next bending corner, and in a second both the field and the distant scarecrow were now gone. I continued my journey and arrived at my new job an hour earlier than expected, just as old John had said.

And what of my first day at work? Well, though the day was long and tiring (I had been out of work so long I had forgotten what it felt like to be active for most of the day), I found I enjoyed being back among human beings again. Come 6:30 I was making my way home, though I took the main road back, given the traffic was never as thick on the evening return as it was in the morning. After all, the rush hour was over by then, and most people were already back home doing the things that people do of an evening.

The next morning, having slept very well and seamlessly through the night, I repeated the pattern of dressing early, putting on the radio, eating some toast, and then following old John's route every turn and curve of the way. I passed down the same roads, the same back streets, before coming once more to the field with the scarecrow. Only this time, I found that the scarecrow was no longer at the very far end against the fence. No. Now it was about half way into the field, again leaning to one side, but much clearer to me. I could see that the body was clad in black, perhaps wearing a dress, though I still couldn't tell. The face of the scarecrow was obscured by the fact it was facing slightly away from me, but I could see it was pale, sheet white, with black hair perhaps sown on to it. Though I presumed it was just a scarecrow, there something unnerving about it, if not, dare I say so, scary. Looking at it and finding it near impossible to look away, I stared at the scarecrow until I turned the corner and it was finally impossible to do so.

The image of that figure, clad in black, leaning slightly, rather like one of those dead people propped up in old photographs, face to one side, stuck with me for the rest of the day, and I found myself distracted while at work, thinking of that lifeless body in the middle of the dark green field.

That night I returned once again by the main road and got home by around 7, making myself some food before settling down on the sofa. I read a little, then ate my food, before relaxing in front of the TV. I had a pleasant night, but in the back of my mind was the figure, the thing I presumed was a scarecrow.

The next day, once again after showering and eating some toast, the radio on in the background, I took the same route, John's instructions becoming more crumpled as the days went by, but his bold handwriting clear as ever.

And once again, around ten minutes into my journey, I came to that field. At first I couldn't see the scarecrow. It seemed to have been taken away; or, as I thought rather macabrely to myself, it had wandered off. My eyes scanned the field but it was nowhere in sight. I couldn't help but feel oddly disappointed, though I have no idea why.

So I drove on, eyes still on the field. And it was then that I saw it, the figure being all of a sudden terrifyingly clear to me now. I saw for the first time that the scarecrow was not a scarecrow at all.

It was in fact a woman, a woman dressed in old Victorian style clothing; a drab black dress with a frilly white collar. Her hair was dark, not quite black but dark grey, and it was pinned back in the old fashioned way. I couldn't believe what I was seeing, but I had to believe it - quite simply because I was seeing it. The logic was undeniable.

And then I saw her face, the face that was looking at me, her eyes dull but at the same time penetrative, staring right into mine with genuine hate in them, her angry expression sending a shiver up my spine. I looked back at her, the woman who stood by the roadside, and I realised that her body was half transparent, and that through her dress I could see the field behind her, the deep green grass merging with her ghostly frame. She was there, but also not there, looking at me with deep intensity. After a second or two as I passed her, my car slowing down almost naturally, her expression began to change, and I got the impression that I clearly wasn't the person she was waiting for or expecting. Now, with this in mind, I saw her disregard me. As soon as she realised I was a stranger and perhaps not the man she awaited, she averted her gaze, her anger fading away to indifference. And then I turned the corner, leaving behind the lady in the field at the road side, to continue looking out for whoever she was looking out for, the man she was hoping would come her way.

I spent much of that morning feeling rather unwell, and more than a little shaken up. I didn't mention what I had seen to my colleagues for obvious reasons, but at lunch time I came over ill and was sick at my desk. Social suicide in one action. I said I'd had some dodgy fish for dinner the previous night, and my manager sent me home. I drove back down the main road, which was thankfully smooth and free of traffic. I simply couldn't even think of going down the country roads.

As I reached my home, old John was standing outside in his front garden, looking listless and feckless. He's one of those old fellows who spent the decades counting down the days, the minutes, the seconds even, to retirement, and then finds himself in his twilight years bored out of his skull with nothing to do but drink and pace the garden. He saw me coming up the drive and cheerfully smiled at me. About to wave at me, he lowered his arm slowly with worry on his face, and his smile faded.

"Oh dear," he said, "you look bloody awful. Are you all right? You're so pale!"

"Yes, I'm fine," I said, not stopping to speak and heading straight for my door with keys in hand. "Some dodgy fish last night. Gonna go straight to bed I think."

He began telling me a story about how he'd had some bad fish in Scarborough in the seventies while on holiday, but I kind of zoned out and interrupted his far from riveting tale by telling him I just had to get inside and lie down. He accepted this and told me to wrap up with a blanket, put the telly on and just relax. I said I would take his advice.

I spent the rest of the day on the sofa, the TV on quietly, but I couldn't relax. I just kept thinking about the woman at the side of the road, her face, how it went from angry to indifferent in a matter of seconds. Every time I closed my eyes to sleep, I saw her face, in extreme close up, half transparent as she had been in the field, the grass visible through her pale face. Eventually I did get to sleep and if I dreamed of the ghostly figure at all, I had no memory of her when I awoke the next morning, still curled up on the sofa like a divorced dad relegated to settee status.

The next day I felt much better, thankfully, and after getting dressed and eating some dry toast, I drove to work. I had no intention of going the back road route and stuck to the main road. Unfortunately this meant I would be stuck in traffic for an hour and a half, maybe even two, but that was preferable to seeing her again.

Over the next few weeks I worked Monday to Friday. Everyday I went by the main road, setting off earlier to get there on time. I built up good relationships with my co-workers and even began dating one of them, Anna, a pretty girl in accounting. We would go out on evenings and alternately stay at each other's houses. It was pleasant, the best relationship I had had in years... well, ever, actually.

One day, about six months after the incident with the woman by the roadside, I awoke later than usual. Turning to my alarm clock I saw that it had gone off. Closer inspection showed me it had been unplugged at the wall. How this had happened I did not know. Whatever had occurred, whether it was me who unplugged it or not, I only had about half an hour to get to work. I slid on my clothes and went straight for the door, having no time for news or breakfast. Instinctively I got into my car, revved the engine up and set off for the back route, through the winding country roads and past the imposing trees which lined them. Naturally, I eventually came close to the field. It had escaped my mind before then, but then I was reminded of her, the woman by the side of the road.

As I reached the field, that chilling place with the dark green grass, I saw a figure at the side of the fence in the distance. Again, it was a figure in black with a white face, but this time I could see it was clearly a scarecrow, just an ordinary scarecrow propped up against the fence, its rags hanging on to the barb wire, the grass creeping up its legs. The field itself still gave me an unsettling feeling, but there was no longer the same atmosphere, and the woman, of course, was nowhere to be seen.

Had I imagined her all along? Or had I actually seen her, waiting as she was for the person that would never arrive? Had she given up her waiting now, and gone off to some other place, the great beyond perhaps? I didn't know. I never mentioned my sighting to anyone. I was about to tell Anna one night, but I decided against it. Besides, it was best to leave it alone. But I still think of her from time to time, the woman at the road side, now a scarecrow in a hidden-away field in the country, and the way her face went from anger to indifference.

THE SINGING SPIRIT

Looking back is an odd thing. It can bring up feelings of nostalgia, often misguided, a sense that one might be gazing into the past with rose tinted spectacles. We are all guilty of recalling the old days and focusing primarily on the good times, the laughs, and ignoring the darkness. For this recollection, against my own character I am forced to bring to attention something that is not exactly dark, but so alien and unexplainable that it fills me with unease. I also feel rather stupid recounting the event, but as this is the way I remember it, there is not much I can do to make logical an occurrence that seems to be so irrational.

As I write this account of the experience I went through, and still cannot believe I really did, my life has transformed into something so different and unrecognisable from how it was that it feels as if I am writing about the account of another person. I'm at my desk here, typing away on something, as images of Marlene Dietrich, as always lit from above, play on the television with no sound. It's the day time, cold but sunny. From where I sit I can see a sleeping cat sprawled on the sofa beside me; outside I see the face of a rabbit, enclosed in his hutch, sipping water fiendishly from his suspended bottle, paws clinging to the metallic grids before him. The rest of the room is dimly lit, but the corner where I type away is illuminated by a lamp which hangs from a wire on the ceiling. As it swings very slightly, eerily so, the light shines through its multi coloured crystals and paints the wall behind it in a rainbow of strange warped patterns.

I am writing now about my present state, a cosy and complacent life with a wife and child in a pleasant home. The time I am looking back to seems like a hell in comparison, some dark cloud I was temporarily trapped in, and seeing as though I could not see through the fog, I was convinced I would remain shrouded in it forever. In those days I lived in a damp, rather grotty basement flat. There was a living room and kitchen in one, with one small window overlooking the yard which belonged to my landlady who lived above me. Strangely, I spent many a day hearing her clumsy foot steps above me, thuds of varying volume depending on the time of day and level of her inebriation. She held the controls to the heating in my poky flat, and as she was a skin flint of the strictest order, she insisted on keeping the radiators off. This meant many a strange night was spent in foisty bath robes, hunched on the sofa which had seen better days decades ago, with a blanket and a hot drink as the TV flickered away in the ever dim room. Even with the lights on, or by the rather pathetic glow of the one lamp I had in the corner, it was a gloomy, rather miserable place to live. In the winter the pipes often froze, and oh so cold it became in December and January. It felt almost like a Dickensian life, living alone in that dank basement.

The living room led its way into a bedroom which felt unsuitable for human slumber. There was a bed in the corner which hid half rotting walls, green at the bottom with mould; over it, a small, almost pointless window, over which hung a veil, yellowing with age. The view from that 12 by 12 square of glass was pitiful at best. From my basement I stood on the bed and gazed through at the streets outside on ground level, but shoes of varying size, colour and type were all one could hope to see. I rarely saw a face but at least kept up with foot wear fashions throughout the time I lived, or should I say existed, in those depressing lodgings.

I rarely had visitors, save for my dad who remained the one anchor to reality, and maybe a friend or two. I lived alone in a kind of state of denial; a denial of loneliness, denial of hopelessness, a denial of the fact I was living a meaningless life. In the winter the place was hopelessly drab. As it was dark by four, I found myself alone surrounded by blackness. Out front, the one light illuminated the street. All to be seen were the bodiless feet which occasionally, but less frequently as the night went on, passed me by, the only sounds being of creaking leather and steps which echoed eerily off the pavement. Out my kitchen window, over which hung a lacy red curtain which really belonged in a sleazy bordello, I saw nothing but a pitch black world. The back garden had no lighting in it, and for all I knew there could have been an army of faces peering in through the window, breathing their unwanted pants of desperation on the glass. One night I heard a noise and went out, only to see a figure fleeing into the darkness. I did not see their face, but saw their back, hunched over in the night, their feet tapping as they left down the winding snicket which led to my somewhat pathetic home.

It was often a very unsettling place to live. Bangs could be heard upstairs when my landlady was not in. As her work often took her out of town for days on end, and she had other properties to tend to, she was infrequently there... which made the sounds from upstairs even more odd. Once when I heard a rather loud bang, I ran outside to go round front and see if there were intruders upstairs. I was shocked to see there wasn't. The lights were off, the windows closed and the front door locked tight. What made life there even weirder was the fact that there was a staircase leading from her house to my basement flat, a locked door separating both at the top, which wasn't lit and was only covered by a flimsy curtain. Often, unsettlingly so, the door would open and when I pulled the curtain back, I would be faced with the sight of my landlady's kitchen... with no one inside it. Who then, I asked myself, was opening the door?

One night, a long and seemingly endless night of which there were many, there was a knock on my door. I sat still and eventually turned my head. There was a silence; then another knock. I stood up cautiously and stepped across the room. Eventually I plucked up the courage to open the door, my hand shaking as I did so. Who was this? Was this the end of my life? Did some crowbar toting thug stand in the night, ready to knock me out cold and empty my flat of the hoarded video cassettes and old crockery, leaving me on the floor with a cracked skull. My imagination had run wild of course and I needn't have feared, for it was my land lady; though one could argue that for any tenant the arrival of the landlady is more terrifying than any intruder could ever be. No, but here she was, looking rather glum, her features lit up by next door's kitchen light which shone from their window and on to her rigid, angular, prominent chinned, almost witch-like face.

"Hi," I said, whimpering slightly, "Is everything OK?"

She wasn't here to talk about the heating, the pipes or, god forbid, the rent, but in fact was informing me of the tragic news of the death of her father. I said I was sorry and put my hand on her shoulder in an attempt to comfort her. After a moment of exchanging words, me of sympathy, she of fond recollection, she asked if I would be able to nip upstairs for a moment. As his funeral was already planned out, she wondered if I might log on to her laptop to download some of her dad's favourite old songs, which, of course, were to be played at his funeral. Immediately I said yes and followed her up the sharp staircase outside, with the black sky overhead, towards the back door, at the top of which led to her kitchen.

We passed through into her living room, where a Picasso imitation dominated a whole wall. It was a portrait, maybe of Dora Maar, but I recall those sharp eyes staring at me as I took a seat and she made me a cup of tea in the kitchen. Putting the lap top on my knee, she asked me to get the music she desired. The song and singer in question had in fact been her father's favourite. I wish I remembered the name of both, but they have slipped into time; I do know it was a popular crooner from the 1930s and 40s. I logged in and began a search on iTunes. Much to her delight and surprise, in a matter of moments I had found it, the exact version she'd been after. We clicked on the preview switch and made double sure it was the right song. It was, and she was so pleased she almost wept. She passed me a hot tea and as I sipped it I began the download. There was a silence, and in the time it took to get the song on her lap top she told me her dad loved to sing this song when she was a child. He even recorded himself on cassette crooning along, much to the household's collective embarrassment.

Finally, it downloaded. She was delighted.

"Let's give it a listen," I said. I pressed play and the song began to whimper, rather meekly, from the lap top. I put it down to the size of the tiny little built in speaker, but I do recall it sounded extremely odd. I can't quite describe it really; very tinny, quite bad quality really for an MP3, and sounding as if someone had just put a microphone to a Hi-Fi speaker and recorded the sound on to tape. The voice singing over the muffled backing track was much too loud too, almost unsettling and unfitting to the sounds. I thought nothing of it at the time, putting it down to a bad quality recording from its vintage era and turned it off.

"There you go," I said, or something to that effect, as I sipped the rest of my tea and placed the cup on the table by my side. My landlady had gone rather quiet, but I shrugged off her pale silence. I presumed she was feeling emotional, hearing her father's favourite song and thinking that she would never see him again. As a younger man, I felt uncomfortable and didn't do much to ease her upset. These days I like to think I'd have more of an idea what to do in such a situation, but my reaction back then was to sigh, get up and prepare myself to leave her to her grief.

"Right," I said, walking away.

"Thanks for that," she said, rather blankly, distracted.

Without another word, and feeling slightly unsettled, I left her house and closed the door behind me. As I descended the staircase to the garden, I peered in through the window and saw my landlady. She was standing still in the same spot, as if frozen, and the sight of her sent a shiver up my spine. Quickly I speeded down the stairs. I could easily have fallen as nothing was lighting them, but thankfully I made it to bottom, when I rushed inside my flat and locked the door behind me.

That night I recall feeling rather odd. I kept thinking of her haunted face, those distant eyes gazing into nothing. I thought of the strange, other worldly music, the distant feel of the crooner. Something about the whole situation unsettled me. Eventually I drifted to sleep on the sofa, my TV on in the background to fill the undesired silence of another long night.

It doesn't end there though. I awoke the next day and had forgotten about the strange incident, and went about my life, as it were. A night or two later, my land lady knocked on my door once again and asked me to come back up to see if I could burn the song on to a disc so she could show me it on the big speakers. There was a look in her eye, almost scheming. I couldn't put my finger on it, but she had a knowing about her. It was as if she was in on some private joke and I had yet to be told about it.

I followed her once again up the staircase, only this time it was the middle of the day, so I was not haunted by unseen faces that may or may not have gazed at me from behind the overgrown ivy which made its way up and around the garden shed. I followed her in and took out a blank disc, on which I burned, quite speedily, the song for her father's funeral.

"Here we are," I said, holding it up with a forced smile.

She stared back at me.

"Put it in the Hi Fi," she said, half smiling. The atmosphere felt strangely sinister. Stiffly I turned around and placed the CD into the player. Then the music sounded up. There, once again, was that ill fitting voice balling over the music. It had sounded odd before, but came across as even more bizarre through the large speakers. Something didn't make sense. I looked to the land lady and saw her warm smile. She looked off into the distance, as if recalling a cherished memory. I was soon to discover what the memory was.

Much to my surprise, my land lady began to explain that the voice I could hear jarringly singing over the track was none other than her father's. As she had told me a few night's previously, when he was younger he had a habit of recording himself singing over his favourite songs on to cassettes. Now I don't know how this happened, but somewhere in the process of me downloading the track and getting it on to her hard drive, her father's voice had inserted itself within. We could not explain it. It didn't scare me as such as I knew he meant no harm, if it indeed was he that did it, and was probably finding a way to send a message to his daughter. Also, the smile on her face showed me that the supernatural, if one believes in it, is not always to be feared. If that is truly what this experience was, a message from beyond the grave, then there was no reason for my land lady to be spooked; or me, for that matter. But if I were to say it wasn't strange, perhaps the most baffling experience of my life, then I would be lying.

Slightly unsettled I have to say, I returned down stairs to my flat and couldn't help but feel glad she had invited me up in the day time, and not waited until the gloomy dark night before revealing the audible visitation from her father. Still, something about hearing such a macabre recording in the afternoon seemed even stranger. One expects chills and scares to occur in the blackness and stillness of the night, for it seems the ideal atmosphere for such goings on. One does not suspect such an occurrence could happen by day light. The rays of sun make it more dreamlike.

A matter of weeks later, my land lady apparently met a spiritual medium. Right away, the medium said:

"Your father is here."

My land lady expressed comfort that he was present.

"He's laughing," said the medium.

"Why?" asked my land lady.

"Because of that song the other week," she replied. "It really scared that young lad..."

If I had been unsettled in that flat before this incident, I was even more uncomfortable after it. I often had nightmares of faces peering through the windows, of her father walking around upstairs, or descending the dark staircase behind the curtain in the corner of my room. I have to say I never saw or heard anything unexplainable there again, but for me, that experience was enough to convince me that, yes, there is something beyond our understanding, and frustratingly so, it will remain just that....

It also convinced me that finding somewhere else to live was a very good idea.

ABOUT CHRIS WADE

Chris Wade is a UK based writer, filmmaker and musician. As well as running the acclaimed music project Dodson and Fogg, he has written books on Marcello Mastroianni, Pablo Picasso, Bob Dylan, John Atkinson Grimshaw, Federico Fellini, and many others. He has also released audiobooks of his comedic fiction, such as Cutey and the Sofaguard, narrated by Rik Mayall. His edits Scenes: The Classic and Cult Film Publication, and for his various projects he has interviewed such people as Sharon Stone, Jeff Bridges, Stacy Keach, Catherine Deneuve, Debbie Harry, Oliver Stone, Stephen Frears, James Woods, Donald Sutherland, and Bertrand Blier. His films include The Apple Picker and he's made documentaries on George Melly, Orson Welles and others.

More info at his website:
wisdomtwinsbooks.weebly.com